Tooth Fairy Travels

FAIRY SCHOOL

Tooth Fairy Travels

by Gail Herman

illustrated by Fran Gianfriddo

A Skylark Book

New York · Toronto · London · Sydney · Auckland

RL 2.5, 006–009

TOOTH FAIRY TRAVELS

A Bantam Skylark Book / June 1999

Skylark Books is a registered trademark of Bantam Books, a division of Random House, Inc. Registered in U.S. Patent and Trademark Office and elsewhere.

ISBN 0-553-48679-9

Published simultaneously in the United States and Canada

Bantam Books are published by Bantam Books, a division of Random House, Inc. Its trademark, consisting of the words "Bantam Books" and the portrayal of a rooster, is Registered in U.S. Patent and Trademark Office and in other countries. Marca Registrada. Bantam Books, 1540 Broadway, New York, New York 10036.

PRINTED IN THE UNITED STATES OF AMERICA

CWO   0   9   8   7   6   5   4   3   2

For Elizabeth

Chapter 1

It was a beautiful day in Fairyland Meadow. Waterfalls sparkled like diamonds. Flowers tall as trees reached up to the sky. Hummingbirds hummed and sunbeams danced.

Tiny Belinda Dentalette waited for her friends beneath the shady cover of a weeping willow tree. She was so excited, her wings fluttered a million beats a second. She

1

peeked out between the long, droopy branches. Ladybugs and butterflies darted here and there, chattering away. The meadow bustled with activity.

"Hello!" Belinda called to the world.

"Hello!" the world called back.

"Hey, Belinda! Where are Trina and Dorrie and Olivia?" Daisy asked, waving her pretty petals hello. She was a fun flower, and the fairies played with her lots of times.

"They'll be here soon," Belinda answered. "Tomorrow is the very first day of Fairy School, so we have lots to talk about!"

Suddenly a big teardrop plopped on her head. The weeping willow was crying! Belinda patted his trunk. "Don't be sad, Mr. Willow," she soothed the tree.

"But I'll miss you fairies when you're in school all day. Who will play under my branches and keep me company?" the tree sobbed.

2

"Don't worry, Mr. Willow. We'll come here after school—unless we have too much homework."

"Promise?"

"Of course. After all, this meadow is practically the only place I can find all by myself."

"Thanks, Belinda," the tree said with a smile. "I feel much better."

Belinda got so excited thinking about school that she started jumping up and down. Her fluttering wings carried her high into the air.

"Hey! Don't fly away!" cried a familiar voice.

Dorrie! Belinda turned to see the branches part. Her friend Dorrie Windmist tumbled into the shade of the tree.

"Oops!" Dorrie rolled to a stop and brushed the dirt off her wings.

Dorrie could be a little clumsy. Sometimes

Belinda worried that Dorrie would bump into something and pop!

"Are you okay?"

"Sure," Dorrie said cheerfully. She scooted next to Belinda and grinned.

Just then the branches parted again. Two more fairies—Trina Larkspur and Olivia Skye—swooped under the tree. "Are we late?" asked Trina.

"Hi, Trina. Hi, Olivia." Belinda grinned. "No, you're right on time. Dorrie just got here. And I left my tree-house early, in case I got lost." Belinda pretended to squint at Trina. "You know, Trina," she added, "I can hardly see you behind that stack of books. And we don't even have homework yet!"

Trina shifted her books to one arm. She brushed her bangs from her eyes. "You know me. I like to be prepared."

4

Trina sounded so serious! She was such a bookworm, Belinda knew she'd be one of the top students at Fairy School.

"I can't believe we're tall enough to go to school," Belinda told her friends. "Three inchworms high! Big enough for first grade!"

"I can't wait for art classes," Olivia said. Her blond hair covered paint smudges on her cheek. Paintbrushes poked out of her back pocket. She bent close to the willow tree's branches and began to braid them into a pretty design.

"What kind of fairy do you think you'll be?" asked Belinda. "A rainbow painter? A cloud shaper?"

"I don't know." Olivia shrugged. "There are so many choices. But we're only just starting. I won't have to decide until we graduate, and that's a long time away."

"Twelve season changes, or 1,085 sunrises," put in Trina.

Dorrie flapped her wings impatiently. "I don't even want to think about graduating— we're just getting started!"

Belinda tickled Dorrie's colorful wings. They were small and sturdy, and they stretched like rubber bands, like all fairy children's wings.

"Don't you want to do real fairy work— like granting wishes or mixing rain-sprinkles?" Belinda asked. "And earn your silver wings?" Belinda loved grown-up silver wings. Glittering, light-as-air wings that sparkled in sunlight, moonlight, and star-light.

"I can't wait to be a tooth fairy," she added. "Just like my mom and dad."

Trina shook her head. "You always talk about being a tooth fairy, Belinda, but are you really sure that's what you want? You'll have to find all those Earth-Below homes. And you always get lost around Fairyland."

"I'm sure I'll be better at finding my way around once school starts," said Belinda. She jumped with excitement. "I'm going to be the best tooth fairy ever."

Just then a loud voice interrupted the friends. "Out of my way, Robin!"

"That sounds like Laurel," Trina whispered. "If we stay quiet, maybe she won't know we're here."

"Did I hear Belinda Dentalette say she wants to be a tooth fairy?" The voice got louder, and another little fairy poked her head under the tree.

"I guess she already knows," Belinda sighed.

Laurel was a fairy just their height. She was always bossing smaller fairies around, and she could be awfully mean to bugs and flowers. Belinda once saw her plucking the petals off a daffodil—even after the flower asked her to stop.

Laurel barged through the curtain of willow branches. "I've got news for you, Ms. I-Want-to-Be-a-Tooth-Fairy." She pointed at Belinda. "I'm going to be a tooth fairy too. So you'd better watch out. Because I'm going to be the best tooth fairy in our class!" The mean fairy stuck out her tongue, turned around, and flew away.

"Owww!" Mr. Willow yelped. "She pulled my leaves." The tree started to cry again. "She's not very nice, is she?"

"She's not nice at all," Dorrie said. She took out a tissue and wiped some of his leaves. "Don't cry, Mr. Willow. You're getting us all wet."

"I almost feel like crying now too," Belinda said. "Laurel is such a bully."

"You can't let Laurel bother you, Belinda," Trina reasoned. "So what if she wants to be a tooth fairy? Plenty of fairies are in the tooth business. She's just jealous because everyone in your family is a tooth fairy."

Belinda thought for a second. Her mother and father were tooth fairies. Her grand-fairyparents, her great-grandfairyparents, and her great-great-grandfairyparents were tooth fairies too. Of course Belinda would be a great tooth fairy. Laurel couldn't change that.

"You're right. Laurel doesn't scare me."

Still, Laurel could really spoil a fairy's fun, Belinda thought.

Olivia, meanwhile, hugged the weeping tree until he stopped crying. "I'm all wet!" she said. "Maybe we should go home and get ready for tomorrow. Let's meet at Fairy Square and fly to school together."

"Good idea," Trina said. Then she turned to Belinda. "Do you want me to fly by your house tomorrow morning so you don't get lost?"

Belinda almost said yes. But she'd been to the Square lots of times. And tooth fairies had to get places on their own. "That's okay," she told Trina. "I think I can get there by myself." Then she flapped her wings, soaring past the others. "See you tomorrow!"

Chapter 2

Belinda flew into the kitchen of her tree-home early the next day. "Good morning, Grandfairy."

"Good morning, princess. I made your favorite breakfast," Grandfairy Dentalette said as she placed a shell-plate in front of Belinda.

"Fairy Dust French Toast? Yummy!" Belinda sat at the tree-stump table while

Grandfairy sprinkled sugar as if she were scattering fairy dust.

Grandfairy Dentalette was a retired tooth fairy. She lived with Belinda and her parents and helped out around the tree.

"Your first day of school!" Grandfairy sighed. "It seems like yesterday I sent your father off. He was such a good student! He took to tooth fairy class like a fish to water. And your mother had the highest tooth grades in her class!"

Belinda listened to Grandfairy talk about their family. How Great-uncle Carl had discovered a baby dinosaur tooth. How a Big Person had almost seen her cousin Danielle before she could sprinkle fairy dust and turn into a butterfly.

"Hi, honeycakes! I'm home!" Mr. Dentalette flew into the tree-house.

"Hi, Dad!" Belinda raced over for a

hug. "Do you think Mom will be back soon?"

"I'm here too!" Mrs. Dentalette announced. She darted into the kitchen, then put down a small suitcase. "I wouldn't miss your first day of school for anything!" She sounded as excited as Belinda felt.

"French toast for everyone!" Grandfairy declared.

Mrs. Dentalette smiled. "Before you know it, Belinda, you'll be a tooth fairy too. We can go on assignments together! A mother-daughter team!"

Belinda smiled back. She imagined flying to Earth-Below, collecting teeth from Little Big People and leaving money under their pillows, then flying home through the big world and back to friendly Fairyland. She wanted to be a tooth fairy so she could work outdoors, soaring and diving, and be fast and strong.

"Last night I stopped at the Big Dipper for a drink of Star Soda," Mrs. Dentalette continued. "The view is so wonderful, all the tooth fairies go there. You turn right at the North Star. . . ."

Belinda listened closely as her mother gave directions. All those lefts and rights and ups and downs! It sounded pretty complicated. She admired her mom for knowing the route so well. Soon Belinda would be zooming around on deliveries too! All she needed were a few easy lessons.

She couldn't wait for school to begin!

"I'm ready to go," she announced, finishing her French toast. Quickly she put her books in a special fairypack shaped like a baby tooth.

"Wait," her mother said. "We have a little gift for you. To celebrate your first day of school." She held out a glittering piece of jewelry.

"A star necklace!" Belinda exclaimed. "Just like real tooth fairies have!"

"Yes. I saw the star on my way home and thought how much you'd like it. So a shooting-star fairy lassoed it up, and I pulled it to the Magic Minimall to have it shrunk."

"Since you want to be a tooth fairy," Mr. Dentalette added, "this will help light your way!"

Belinda clasped the star necklace around her neck. "Thanks, Mom and Dad. I'll never take it off."

She kissed everyone good-bye.

"Have fun in school!" called Mrs. Dentalette as Belinda flew outside. The little fairy circled the tree, then took off down Magic Carpet Avenue, flying past a chirping bird.

"Good morning, Mrs. Sparrow," Belinda

said. "I'm off to Fairy Square to meet my friends for our first day of school."

"Well then, you're going the wrong way, dear!" the sparrow told her. "You take Pixie Skyway to the Enchanted Crossing to get to Fairy Square."

Belinda groaned. Turned around again!

Chapter 3

Belinda hurried along Pixie Skyway. Good thing she was one of the fastest fairies in Fairyland. She sped past Moonlight Mall to the Enchanted Crossing. Now I'm moving! she thought. Up ahead, she spied Fairy Square. Olivia and Trina waited near the Fairy Godmother Statue.

"Hi, you two," Belinda called down to her friends. "Looks like Dorrie is even later than I am."

Belinda hovered in the air, too excited to land.

"Hey," Olivia said. "Is that a star necklace? Come down so I can see it!" She shielded her eyes from the strong starlight as Belinda fluttered to the ground.

"My mom gave it to me," Belinda told her friends proudly.

Olivia examined the necklace. "It seems to be especially twinkly," she said.

Olivia knew so much about art and design. When she gave you a compliment, it really meant something.

"Thanks," Belinda said, smiling.

Just then the three friends heard a loud flapping noise. They looked up and saw Dorrie circling above them.

"Watch out below!" she shouted. "I'm coming in for a landing!"

"Be careful, Dorrie!" Belinda called. "You're heading right for—"

"Oof!" Dorrie grunted as she dropped onto the Fairy Godmother Statue. She got tangled up in the statue's long cape, and she looked very surprised.

Belinda giggled. "Need some help?" she asked.

"Yes, please," Dorrie said as her friends flew up. Belinda took one hand, Trina the other, and Olivia guided Dorrie's wings.

For a moment, the friends hung in the air and talked about school.

"I hope we get magic wands," Dorrie said.

"I hope we have lots of art classes," Olivia added.

"I hope the library has tons of great books," Trina put in.

"I hope I learn how not to get lost," Belinda said cheerfully.

The school bell chimed in the distance. Belinda took a deep breath. "Ready?" she asked.

"Ready!" said her friends.

Seconds later, the four fairies flew into the first-grade branch of the school-tree. Their teacher hovered in front of the class.

"Welcome, first-grade fairies," she said. "I'm Ms. Periwinkle. Take a seat and we'll get started."

Belinda slid into a chair next to Olivia, behind Trina and Dorrie. She almost frowned when she saw Laurel fly to a toadstool desk right behind her. But Belinda was too excited to be bothered. "School is going to be the best!" she whispered to Olivia.

"All right, class. Let's start the day by singing our fairy pledge," Ms. Periwinkle said.

Belinda looked at her friends. They all loved to sing, and the fairy pledge was their favorite song. School was fun already!

We are fairies
Brave and bright.
Shine by day,
Twinkle by night.

We're friends of birds
And kind to bees.
We love flowers
And the trees.

We are fairies
Brave and bright.
Shine by day,
Twinkle by night.

"And now," Ms. Periwinkle continued when they were done singing, "I'd like to talk about what we'll learn."

Belinda sat forward. This was the good part.

"This season, we'll study cloud shaping and flower painting."

Belinda nudged Olivia. Lots of art classes.

Ms. Periwinkle continued. "We'll also study fairy dust throwing, rainbow making, and spell reading."

Trina should like that, Belinda thought.

"And every morning we'll have tooth fairy class. So let's get started."

Tooth fairy class! That was the perfect way to start the day! Belinda opened her notebook.

Olivia grinned at her. "You'll have to help me," she whispered. "I don't know anything about tooth fairies."

Laurel snickered. "I'm not surprised," she said in a nasty voice.

"Shhh." Belinda turned around. How dare Laurel be mean to sweet, gentle Olivia?

"Ms. Periwinkle," Laurel called out quickly. "Belinda is bothering me!"

23

"Girls!" Ms. Periwinkle said. "Quiet down and pay attention."

Belinda turned red. Already in trouble, and it was only the first day!

"Now," Ms. Periwinkle continued, "who knows what tooth fairies do?"

Belinda sat up straight. This was it. The real beginning of her education. And she knew the answer! She could make up for getting yelled at by answering the first question in fairy school right! She flapped one wing to get the teacher's attention.

Ms. Periwinkle smiled. Belinda smiled back, relieved to see that the teacher wasn't mad. "Yes, Belinda?"

"A tooth fairy checks her loose-tooth logbook to find the Little Big People who are going to lose a tooth that day. Then she visits each child on Earth-Below, leaves money under the pillow, and takes the tooth to a special warehouse. Everyone in my family is in the tooth fairy business," Belinda couldn't help adding. "Some of them are famous tooth fairies. I'm going to be a tooth fairy someday too."

"Humph!" Laurel snorted.

"That's very nice," the teacher said, "but you might change your mind and decide to be a different kind of fairy. Who knows? School is just beginning. You may find a class you like better."

"That will never happen," Belinda said softly. "I'm going to be a star tooth fairy."

Ms. Periwinkle didn't hear. "To find the child on Earth-Below," the teacher was saying, "tooth fairies need to read maps."

A stack of papers drifted out from Ms. Periwinkle's desk. One sheet floated to each student. Belinda caught her paper and looked it over. It was a map of Fairyland.

Belinda was nervous. Maps always confused her. Couldn't Ms. Periwinkle start with something else? Like different ways to see in the dark? Or how to hide from Earth-Below children? Those were the fun things. Things Belinda knew she'd be good at.

Why did they have to start with maps?

"For homework, I'd like you to trace the shortest distance from school to Fairy Square," Ms. Periwinkle told the class.

Fairy Square? Belinda had just come from there. "I should know this," she whispered happily.

"Talking to yourself, Belinda?" Laurel sneered. "That's no way for a star tooth fairy to behave!"

Fairy fiddles! Belinda thought. Laurel is nothing but trouble.

Chapter 4

After school, Belinda flew to the Fairyland Meadow pond with her friends. It was so warm that daisies spun their petals to fan the air.

The fairies waved to the weeping willow tree. Then Belinda flew to the top of a waterfall slide. "Last one down is a rotten tooth!" she cried, whooshing down.

Dorrie and Olivia raced after her while

Trina carefully put her books on the ground, away from the water. Then she took off too. The four friends tumbled and splashed, and Belinda zipped to the top of the slide every time her feet touched the ground.

"See you later," Trina called after a little while. "I'm going to the library to do some homework."

Homework! Belinda remembered the tooth fairy assignment. But it was such a nice day, she hated to go inside. "We all have the same homework," she said to her friends. "Why don't we do it together? But let's work right here."

"Good idea," said Trina.

The fairies stepped under the Sun Shower. Warm rays dried their clothes and hair. Belinda spread her Fairyland map open on a toadstool table. "Hmmm," she said. Now that she was looking at the map, find-

29

ing the shortest route to Fairy Square didn't seem so simple after all.

"Will I be the only tooth fairy in history who can't read a map?" Belinda asked, half joking.

"No way!" Trina told her. "You'll get the hang of this in a jiffy."

Belinda gave a little laugh. "That's easy for you to say, Ms. Bookworm. You don't get lost at every turn!"

"Hey!" said Dorrie. "That almost rhymes."

"I've got a good idea," Olivia said. "Let's make a rhyme to help you, so you won't get lost!"

Dorrie giggled. "I've got one! *Roses are red, violets are blue, to help our friends, we stick like glue.*"

"That's very sweet," Olivia said. "That can be our friendship motto."

"I like your idea," Trina agreed. "But it won't help Belinda find her way."

Belinda smiled at her friends. They were trying so hard to help her.

"How about this?" said Olivia. *"Look around and go slow. You'll always know just where to go."*

Belinda's smile faded. She hated to fly slowly.

"Perfect!" said Trina. "Most of the time you get lost because you fly so fast you don't see where you're going. *So remember the rhyme and you'll do fine!"*

Belinda looked at her map. What Trina said made sense. She began to trace a route.

Then a cuckoo-clock bird flew past. "Cuckoo!" it called. "Cuckoo! Cuckoo! Cuckoo!"

"Oh, no!" Belinda groaned. "Four

o'clock! Almost dinnertime." At the Dentalette tree-house, dinner was early so her parents could go to work before dark. "I'd better get going."

"I'm leaving too," Trina told her. "Do you want me to fly with you?"

"No, thanks—I know how to get home from here. See you later, Olivia. Bye, Trina and Dorrie."

***

Mr. and Mrs. Dentalette were setting the table when Belinda finally flew home. Grandfairy stirred a big nutshell filled with angel-hair pasta and toad-stools.

"Hi, honeycakes," said Belinda's dad. He handed her the napkin-leaves. "You're just in time to help. How was school?"

"Tell us all about it," Mrs. Dentalette

32

said, placing the shell-plates around the table.

"It was great," Belinda told them. "Ms. Periwinkle is really nice, and we did all sorts of fun stuff like flower painting. I jumped from Cloud Nine all the way to Cloud Fourteen in gym class."

"That's terrific!" said Mrs. Dentalette.

"Tooth fairy class was fun too," Belinda added. "But we already have a tough homework assignment."

"Do you need any help?" Mr. Dentalette asked. "You know, you have two experienced tooth fairies right here."

"No, thanks," Belinda answered. She was determined to figure out the route on her own.

As she worked on the assignment after dinner, she stared at the map for a long time, but it didn't make sense. *Just look around and go slow,* she reminded herself. She looked at the map again. Wasn't that Fairy Meadow? Yes. And there was Pixie Highway. She traced a path on the map. All done, she thought happily. That wasn't so hard.

Chapter 5

The next morning, Belinda sat at her toad-stool desk, proud of herself. She'd finished her homework, and it hadn't even taken that long.

"Okay, class. Let's have a look at your tooth fairy assignment." Ms. Periwinkle waved her wand. Everyone's sheet floated off their desk to a blank wall on one side of the room. Ms. Periwinkle hovered in front of the papers, examining each one.

"Nice work, Trina," she said. "You too, Sebastian and Clarabelle."

Belinda held her breath. Her map was next. Ms. Periwinkle gazed at the paper, then traced the route with her finger. Belinda squirmed in her seat. Why was she taking so long?

"Well, Belinda," Ms. Periwinkle said, "you do get to Fairy Square. And this would be a great sightseeing trip around Fairyland! But I think there are shorter routes."

Belinda's heart sank. Tooth fairies weren't supposed to give sightseeing tours.

Laurel chuckled behind Belinda while Ms. Periwinkle stopped at the last map and examined it closely. "She's looking at mine now, Belinda. Watch and learn how a real tooth fairy does things."

"I don't believe it!" Ms. Periwinkle flapped her wings excitedly. "Class! Laurel's discovered a new shortcut. She's found the shortest route—ever!"

Laurel tapped Belinda on the shoulder. "Who's the star tooth fairy now?" she sneered.

***

"Try not to feel so bad," Olivia told Belinda a little later. They were in the school meadow painting rainbows.

"I know," Belinda said glumly. "When Ms. Periwinkle explained the shorter routes, it all made sense. But I want to be good at everything that has to do with tooth fairies."

"Maybe a few more classes will help," Olivia said.

Just then Ms. Periwinkle walked by. "Nice work, girls," she said. "You have the curve just right!"

Olivia blushed at the compliment, and Belinda grinned.

Ms. Periwinkle clapped her hands. "Attention, class! We'll be staying in the school meadow a little longer today. The wind is just right for scattering fairy dust."

Fairy dust! Belinda's eyes lit up. That was the strongest kind of fairy magic. Fairy dust could change objects. Make things happen.

Ms. Periwinkle gave each student a special pouch. Then she licked one finger and held it up in the air. "The wind is coming from the northwest. Throw carefully. And remember, your thoughts guide the dust, so be careful what you think."

"Watch out, everybody," Trina announced. "I'm going to try!"

She opened her pouch, scooped up a handful, and tossed her fairy dust high in the sky. It circled the school meadow in large swoops. Finally it landed on her pile of books.

The books danced into the air. They sailed through a knot in a tree trunk and into the school library. Everyone rushed to look inside.

A library stamp bounced off the checkout desk. The books flipped open, and the stamp dropped down on each one.

"They're being renewed!" Belinda shouted.

The books floated back through the window and into Trina's waiting arms.

"That was great, Trina!" Dorrie exclaimed.

"A very strong first try," Ms. Periwinkle said.

Trina beamed. "I was thinking about my books and it just happened!"

Ms. Periwinkle smiled back. "That's how it works."

She opened her grade book and gave Trina an A.

"I'm ready to try now," Dorrie said as she reached into her bag and grabbed two big handfuls. The bag tore in half, and a cloud of dust rose to the sky and flew helter-skelter. Quickly the dust swirled down, down, down. It spun around Dorrie, finally settling on her head.

"Oh, no!" cried Dorrie. "I was thinking about getting my hair cut. What's going to happen?"

It didn't take long to find out.

Dorrie's hair turned purple, then orange, then bright, bright pink. She sighed with relief, looking in a pocket mirror. "That's not too bad," she said. "Pink is kind of cool."

Suddenly one strand of hair stood on end, then another and another, until each and every one towered above her head.

Dorrie gasped in dismay. Belinda raced over. She tried to pat her friend's hair into place, but Dorrie's hair popped back up every time.

Laurel strode over. "Don't worry," she said sweetly. "It won't last very long."

"Really?" asked Dorrie.

"Really," Laurel said. Then she laughed. "Not more than a year or two."

Dorrie moaned, more upset than ever.

"It will be okay, Dorrie," Belinda said. "Right, Ms. Periwinkle?"

"Of course it will," the teacher said. Belinda shot Laurel a look as Ms. Periwinkle walked over.

"Give me one second, Dorrie, and I'll reverse your hair." The teacher reached into her bag. "Hmmm, I don't think I have enough dust here. Wait while I go get more."

"Could I try, Ms. Periwinkle?" Belinda

asked. "I haven't used my fairy dust yet, and I'd like to help out."

Ms. Periwinkle frowned. "Reversing fairy magic is the hardest way to use fairy dust. But why don't you give it a try? You certainly can't hurt Dorrie's hair, and maybe you'll learn a thing or two."

"You can't do it," Laurel whispered nastily. "No way, nohow."

Belinda closed her eyes and ignored Laurel. She thought really hard and imagined Dorrie's hair as it usually looked—kind of messy and curly. She took a deep breath, reached into her bag, and threw the dust into the air. The fairy dust fell like rainbow-sprinkles on Dorrie's hair. For a whole minute, nothing happened.

"You didn't do anything," Laurel said gleefully.

"Don't worry, Belinda. I'll go get more . . ." Ms. Periwinkle stopped talking.

Dorrie's hair was changing . . . turning colors. It went from pink to green to blue to purple to yellow! Finally it stayed brown, just like normal, then dropped down bit by bit into its usual style.

"Whew," said Dorrie, patting her head. "That feels much better."

"Belinda, I'm very impressed," Ms. Periwinkle said. "What you just did takes talent. Reversing a fairy spell is a very advanced skill." She opened her grade book and wrote a great big *A* next to Belinda's name.

Wow, Belinda thought. My first A.

"Too bad you'll never be that good in tooth fairy class!" Laurel sneered when their teacher turned her back.

Chapter 6

The fairies loved school. There was so much to learn and so many new things to try. In spell reading class, Trina made up rhymes so quickly, everyone was amazed. In cloud class, Olivia sculpted a big cloud into the shape of an airplane—a funny flying thing they'd all seen from time to time zooming past Fairyland. Dorrie was learning how to wave her magic wand in wish class without knocking something over. And Belinda was flying faster than anybody in fairy gym. But each morning when Ms. Periwinkle announced tooth fairy class, Belinda got a funny feeling in her stomach.

Sometimes they'd talk about famous tooth fairies. They learned who had picked up the most teeth in a single night, who had been the youngest tooth fairy to go to Earth-Below, who had found the biggest tooth. Those classes were fun. But sometimes they worked on reading maps. And those classes made Belinda very nervous. She hated maps.

One day when class started, Ms. Periwinkle handed directions to each student. "This is a surprise quiz," she explained, "to test your tooth-finding skills. Follow these directions to the end, and I'll be waiting to grade you."

Belinda's heart sank as she glanced at the sheet. "Begin your journey by flying off the tree branch," she read. "Face north and flutter your wings twenty times. Then fly nine wing flaps east to the Butterfly Road. Turn southwest and head toward Strawberry Grove, then somersault backward six times in a row. Pick up one of the teeth hidden under the Lucky Clover. Then return to class."

Ms. Periwinkle smiled at Belinda. "Why don't you go first?" she asked.

Belinda tried to smile back. But her stomach was tied in knots.

Trina flew up to her. "It will be okay," she whispered. "Just remember: *Look around and go slow. You'll always know just where to go.*"

Ms. Periwinkle whisked a stopwatch out of her pocket. Belinda groaned. She couldn't go slow. They were being timed! I have to go fast to get a good grade, she thought.

"Ready . . . set . . . ," the teacher said, pressing the Start button on the watch, "go!"

Belinda took off through the leaves above her class branch. She flew as fast as she could and tried to follow the directions: north, east, southwest. Twenty flutters, nine flaps, and . . . was that Strawberry Grove up ahead?

Wait! Did she need to turn left or right to go southeast? Or was it southwest? She was so confused!

Sighing, Belinda realized she'd have to start over. And this time she'd take it a little more slowly. She turned around to head back to the classroom. Now, where was Fairy School?

Look around and go slow . . . and I'm

still lost, she thought. She was ready to cry. She looked down to hide her tears. Then she noticed something. The Lucky Clover was below her. She'd found the teeth!

Belinda looked around and realized that Fairy School was right behind her! The directions were just one big circle. Belinda grabbed a tooth and raced back to her class as fast as she could fly.

Ms. Periwinkle nodded and pressed the Stop button. "Hmmm," she said. "You found the teeth, but it took a very long time. D-plus."

"D-plus?" Belinda shook her head. "How will I tell my parents?"

Ms. Periwinkle patted Belinda's wing. "Your parents will understand. This is only one tooth test. You're a good student, Belinda. Just look how well you're doing in

other classes. Every fairy can't be good at every fairy subject."

Belinda sighed. "But I have to be good at tooth fairy class," she said.

"Why?" her teacher asked.

"Because . . . Because I have to be a star tooth fairy."

"Do you like tooth fairy class, Belinda?" Ms. Periwinkle asked.

"Well . . ." Belinda couldn't answer her teacher.

"You don't seem to enjoy it. Maybe being a different kind of fairy will make you happy. You're great at speed flying and cloud hopping," Ms. Periwinkle said.

Sure, Belinda had A's in lots of classes. But they weren't tooth fairy class! And she had to be a tooth fairy.

Didn't she?

Laurel went next. Faster than a fairy flip,

she flew to the Lucky Clover and back. "I got an A!" she exclaimed. "I bet I have the fastest time in the whole class! I'm the best tooth fairy in school!"

She did a cartwheel and landed lightly just in front of Belinda. "And you're the worst!"

Chapter 7

The worst tooth fairy? Tears stung Belinda's eyes. She felt as low as a caterpillar. How could she be the worst? She was a Dentalette. She should be the best.

"Don't let that mean little fairy bother you," Olivia told her as the four friends flew out of school at the end of the day. "Laurel doesn't know everything."

Maybe not, Belinda thought. But she

seems to know an awful lot about tooth fairy stuff.

"Listen, everyone," Belinda said. "Do you mind if I don't play today? I feel like going home."

Olivia hugged Belinda. "Of course we don't mind. We'll see you tomorrow. Goodbye."

Belinda couldn't say anything else. She was too afraid she'd cry. She was supposed to be a star tooth fairy, but she had the lowest grades in class! And that horrible Laurel would never let her forget it.

She wished there were something she could do to prove what a good tooth fairy she would be. Something big. Bigger than a homework assignment or surprise quiz. Something that would show Laurel and everyone else that she could be a star.

Belinda slowly flew home.

"Hi, honeycakes. What's wrong?" Mr.

Dentalette asked when he saw her. "You're moving slower than a sleepy snail."

"Hi, Daddy," Belinda said, sniffling. She'd always been able to tell her dad anything. Maybe he could help her now. But how could she tell him she was the worst fairy in her class? He'd be so disappointed. That made her cry harder. "Oh, Daddy," she said. "I feel terrible! I—"

Belinda reached toward the table for a tissue and spied an old photo of her mom. In the picture, Mrs. Dentalette was a smiling teenager, about to go on her first tooth assignment. Suddenly Belinda had a terrific idea, guaranteed to prove what a good tooth fairy she really was. She could go down to Earth-Below and pick up a tooth like a real tooth fairy!

"Yes?" Mr. Dentalette prompted Belinda gently. "You don't feel well?"

"That's right," Belinda told him quickly.

She didn't have to tell her dad about the tooth fairy class after all. She'd go on a real delivery assignment. She could be the youngest tooth fairy to make a delivery. She'd break the record and be famous! A real star tooth fairy. Then no one would care about her grades.

"I think I'm getting a cold. *Achoo!*" Belinda sneezed loudly.

Mr. Dentalette sprinkled fairy dust and the specks clumped together, forming a pill. "Take this pepper pill," he said. "You'll sneeze the cold right out."

A pepper pill? Yuck! But Belinda poured a glass of nectar and swallowed the pill.

"*Aaaaaachoooooo!*" The tree-house shook to its roots.

"There," Mr. Dentalette said. "Feel better?"

"All better!" said Belinda cheerfully. "I'm going to play in the meadow!"

Belinda was so excited about her plan, she couldn't wait to tell her friends.

✳✳✳

"So I'll find a child's house," she told Trina, Dorrie, and Olivia a few minutes later as they sat under the willow's branches, "deliver the money, and take the tooth. I'll go down in Fairyland history as the youngest working tooth fairy ever! Ms. Periwinkle will probably give me extra credit to make up for my bad tooth grade."

Olivia gave Belinda a funny look. "I know tooth fairy class has been hard for you," she said gently. "And you want to do something really great. But how will you know where to go?"

Belinda shrugged. "I'll check my mom's

loose-tooth logbook and find somebody. It's probably easy to read a map when you do it for real. Easier than doing it in school, anyway. Besides, I'm a great flier. That counts for something."

"Of course it counts for something," Dorrie said. "But you never know what can go wrong. Even with simple fairy magic." She patted her hair and gave a little laugh. "And where will you get the money?"

"I'll find a way," Belinda said.

"Tooth fairies need years of training," Trina said matter-of-factly. "It's a serious job. And you haven't finished one tooth class yet!"

"Besides," Dorrie added fearfully, "Big People on Earth-Below are scary. They keep animals as . . . as . . . pets! And Little Big People catch fairies too, and bring them to school for show-and-tell."

"It's not safe for little fairies on Earth-

Below," Olivia said. "Everybody knows the Big People are so tall they can pluck the leaves off the tallest trees. If they jump too hard, they can cause an earthquake!"

Belinda shivered a bit. She didn't believe all those stories. Not really. And she couldn't believe her friends! They thought she couldn't make the delivery. Well, she would just have to surprise them along with everybody else.

"Maybe you're right," she said. "Going down to Earth-Below is a silly idea."

Chapter 8

Belinda ate dinner with her family that night, just like always.

But tonight was going to be different. Belinda was going to make a delivery! She gobbled down her food.

"You're in a hurry," Mrs. Dentalette commented.

"I've got a big assignment," Belinda said. That wasn't quite a lie, she figured. She did have an assignment—just not for school.

"Too bad you have so much homework," Mr. Dentalette said. "Mom and I aren't starting work until later. We thought we could all take a flight around the neighborhood."

"Maybe we could go to the new BeeHive for honey sticks," Grandfairy added.

Belinda sighed. That sounded nice. Maybe her trip could wait.

But no, she realized. This made it so much easier! Her parents kept extra tooth money in a hollow log, and now Belinda could use those quarters! Plus, her mother wouldn't rush off with her logbook. Belinda could take her time and read all the entries. Then she could pick the perfect child.

"You all go ahead," she told her family.

"We can do something special over the weekend."

Like celebrate, she added to herself. Surely her parents would want to throw a party for the youngest tooth fairy ever!

After everyone left, Belinda flipped through her mother's logbook. A boy named James had just lost a tooth. Belinda gazed at the map to his house. A maze of twisty roads curved in all sorts of directions. Too complicated, she decided.

She turned the page. "Emily Ann," she read. "Seven years old. Lives on Bank Street in River View. Loves to be outdoors. Lost her first tooth at 3:35 P.M. playing baseball."

Hmmm. Emily Ann sounded interesting. If she'd been a fairy she might have been one of Belinda's friends.

She checked the map and directions. River View was a small town without many streets. It seemed like an easy delivery. Even for me, Belinda thought as she tore out the map. If she left now, she could be back before her parents went to work. They'd be so pleased when she came home, tooth in hand! They wouldn't care that she'd torn out one little page from the logbook and borrowed money.

Belinda flew to the edge of Fairyland without getting lost once. I'm a better tooth fairy already, she thought as she gazed at the Rainbow Bridge, the entryway to Earth-Below. She'd never slid down before . . . never visited the Big People. The bridge sure looked steep. She trembled.

Right then and there, Belinda almost turned around. This was a very scary adventure. But she had to make this delivery to prove to herself and everybody else that she was a star tooth fairy. *Look around and go slow,* she reminded herself. *You'll always know just where to go.*

She rubbed her star necklace for luck and leaped onto the bridge. *Whoosh!* She slid down the rainbow, slipping this way and that, heading straight for Earth-Below.

Chapter 9

Belinda tumbled off the rainbow and flew down the icy mountain snowcaps that separated Fairyland from Earth-Below. It doesn't look that much different here, she thought. Just . . . bigger. Now, which way? She looked at her map. "Turn right at Big Bear Cloud," she read, "then dive south."

That sounded simple enough. But where was Big Bear Cloud?

"G-r-r-r."

Was that a growl? A roar? The sound a bear would make? Belinda wasn't sure. At home, the bears were friendly. She spun around and saw a big black storm cloud. She gasped. It had sharp cloud claws and pointy cloud teeth!

Frightened, Belinda sped off to the right. Then she plunged down . . . down . . . so fast, she couldn't steer.

"Ouch!" she cried as she bounced off a tree and flipped over. *Thump!* She landed on a soft patch of long green grass.

R-r-r-r. What's that sound? she wondered as she looked around. A Big Person—a real live Big Person who wasn't even big enough to reach the lowest leaf on a tree! Belinda stared in amazement. She was on Earth-Below!

The Big Person was pushing something

that made a terrible noise and spit out broken bits of grass. And Belinda was sitting right in front of its spinning blades! Closer and closer it came. She was going to be sucked inside and shredded into a hundred fairy pieces!

Just in time, Belinda spread her wings. She soared up past the lawn mower and landed on a prickly rosebush.

"Oof!" she exclaimed. She jumped up quickly, then settled down on a petal. "Now I know how Dorrie feels!" she said, laughing.

"Those landings can be killers," a passing bumblebee buzzed.

Belinda managed a smile. "Excuse me," she said, "but is this River View?"

"Yes. What's your buzzness here?" the bee asked politely.

Belinda was about to tell him. She

planned to ask directions to Bank Street too. Then she caught sight of another Big Person bending over the rosebush with a pair of scissors just like the ones Belinda used to cut snowflakes—only a hundred times bigger. The Big Person snipped at the air, moving right toward Belinda!

"Better buzzzz off," the bee said as he zipped away.

Belinda darted behind a big rock. Whew, she thought. Two close calls. Earth-Below was a dangerous place for a little fairy. And everything was so big. It all looked so much smaller on the map. It could take hours to find Emily Ann's house.

Still, here she was in River View. She had found the town easily enough! She just wasn't sure where to go next, and the bumblebee was nowhere to be found.

"Let's see," Belinda said, gazing at her

map. Bank Street was clearly marked with a big red star. "All I have to do is find the street with a big star on it. That should be easy."

Belinda searched high and low for the red star. She flew up and down streets and alleys, over bridges, and through tunnels. But she couldn't find the star.

"Where is it?" she muttered. She peered at the map and looked around her. Nothing seemed to match.

Look around and go slow, she reminded herself. *You'll always know just where to go.*

Maybe if she took her time and explored a little more, she'd stumble onto Bank Street. She could get lucky. Right?

Taking a deep breath, Belinda circled the town. It started to get dark. Thank goodness I have my necklace, she thought as it brightened the night. I wish it could tell me how to get to Bank Street. I don't think I'm ever going to find my way.

Belinda's star necklace lit empty, eerie streets. Strange noises rang through the air. Earth-Below was very scary. Right about now, she knew, her parents were going into her room to say good night. They were opening her door . . . finding her bed empty.

"My friends were right," Belinda said aloud. "This was a silly idea. I'm going home."

She flew high into the starry sky. Now, where was Big Bear Cloud? And the Rainbow Bridge?

"Oh, no!" she groaned. "Which way is home?"

***

Back in Fairyland, Belinda's family flew around in a panic.

"She was here when we left," cried Mrs. Dentalette. "Where could she have gone?"

"Maybe she's with her friends," Grandfairy suggested.

"Of course!" Mr. Dentalette nodded. He waved his wand, and a messenger fairy appeared. "Please find out if Belinda is visiting a friend."

"Sure thing, Mr. Dentalette. Be back in a flash."

Before the Dentalettes could count to ten, the messenger fairy reappeared with Dorrie, Trina, and Olivia tagging along.

"We're worried about Belinda too," Trina said. "We think we know what happened." Quickly she explained Belinda's plan, how she wanted to break a record and be the youngest tooth fairy to pick up a tooth.

"But we didn't think she'd do it," Dorrie interrupted. "She told us she wouldn't go to Earth-Below!"

"Are you sure about this?" Grandfairy asked.

"Almost positive," Olivia said.

Trina snapped her fingers. "Is your loose-tooth logbook missing?" she asked Mrs. Dentalette. "Maybe Belinda took it with her so she could find a child below."

Mrs. Dentalette shook her head. "It's right here."

"Well, maybe we can find a clue in it," Trina said.

Everyone bent over the book.

"Look!" Dorrie exclaimed. "One page is torn out!"

"It's a map page," Mrs. Dentalette said.

She read the entry about Emily Ann on the facing page. "It's the route to a house in River View."

"I know where River View is!" Mr. Dentalette said.

"Come on!" Grandfairy jumped to her feet. "Let's go!"

"We're coming too," Dorrie declared. "But I fly kind of slowly," she added. "And I'm afraid of flying in the dark."

"We'll all stick together," Olivia told her. "Just like our friendship rhyme. Remember, *Roses are red, violets are blue, to help our friends, we'll stick like glue.* Come on!"

Chapter 10

Belinda sat on a dark riverbank in a circle of light from her star necklace. She was lost—and stuck on Earth-Below. Birds squawked. Owls hooted in the tree above her. Strange squeaks and noises echoed through the air. Belinda jumped at every sound.

I'm a terrible tooth fairy. Maybe I'll spend my whole life right here, she thought miserably. Some human will spot me and think I'm a fly. He'll swat me down and I'll never make it home.

Home. That was where Belinda belonged. The little fairy gazed at the big, strange Earth-Below houses and sighed. Right now she didn't care what Laurel—or anyone else—thought about her tooth fairy skills. She just wanted to be in Fairyland.

"If I do make it back," she said to herself, "I won't worry about being the best tooth fairy in school. I won't worry about being a tooth fairy at all! I don't like all this tooth fairy stuff! I hope Mom and Dad won't be too angry."

Sure, she liked flying at night. And sliding down the Rainbow Bridge to Earth-Below was fun. But she could use those skills in other fairy jobs too. And as Ms. Periwinkle had said, Belinda was good at so many other classes. She could be anything she wanted! If only she could get back to Fairy-land . . .

Then Belinda heard another strange sound, a creaking coming from above. She looked up and saw a baby robin perched on the edge of his nest.

That looks awfully dangerous, Belinda thought. She glanced around and saw that the mother robin was many inchworms away, searching for twigs on the ground to add to her nest.

A robin family! Maybe they can help me, Belinda thought.

"Mommy, I'm hungry!" the baby robin sang. He hopped up and down to get his mother's attention, but she was too far away to see or hear him. As Belinda watched, the little bird lost his balance. He swayed left and right, flapping his wings, but he didn't know how to fly yet. He toppled out of the nest!

"Mommy!" the baby cried as he fell.

"Robbie!" shrieked the mother as she hurried after him.

The tiny bird was hurtling to the ground. His mother was too far away. She'd never reach him in time. Belinda had to do something—quick! Without another thought she flew up, up, up, moving faster than lightning. She caught the baby robin and held him tight in her arms. A second later, the mother robin flew over.

"Thank you," she sang as she wrapped her wings around her little bird and hugged him close. "You flew so fast. I never would have reached him in time!"

Belinda smiled. The baby robin was safe with his mother, and she was glad. Now if only Belinda could get back to *her* mommy. She opened her mouth to ask directions.

"Belinda . . ."

Belinda whirled around. Was someone calling her name? She strained to listen. There! She heard it again.

"Belinda . . . Belinda Dentalette."

"Mommy?" Belinda jumped to her feet. "I'm here! By the robin's nest!"

"Belinda!" Mrs. Dentalette hovered by the branch. "I saw your star light!" She hugged Belinda tight.

A moment later Grandfairy flew over with Mr. Dentalette and Belinda's friends.

"You found me!" Belinda exclaimed.

"Thanks to Trina, Olivia, and Dorrie," Mr. Dentalette said. "They told us about your plan."

"Well," Belinda said with a sigh, "it wasn't much of a plan. I'm a tooth fairy failure—"

"Excuse me," the mother robin interrupted Belinda. "I would like to tell you something, young fairy. You may not be good at collecting teeth, but you are *not* a failure. You saved my little bird's life. And I've never seen a bird or bug fly faster than you. I'd say that's all pretty successful!"

Belinda blushed.

"We're so proud of you, Belinda," Mr. Dentalette said with a big smile.

"Even though I'm a bad tooth fairy?"

"Oh, honeycakes," Mr. Dentalette said. "We don't care what kind of fairy you are. As long as you're a happy one."

Mrs. Dentalette hugged Belinda tight. "We're proud of you, no matter what. As long as you always try your best, that's good enough for us."

Belinda grinned. Her parents didn't care if she wasn't a tooth fairy! She was so happy she felt as if she could burst. She didn't even care if Laurel made fun of her every day for being a bad tooth fairy. Belinda was good at other things, and that was every bit as important.

"Well," she said with a laugh, "I guess there won't be a party now."

"A party?" Mrs. Dentalette repeated. "What do you mean?"

"I thought there might be a celebration. You know, once I broke a tooth fairy record."

Her parents looked at each another. "We can still have a party," Mrs. Dentalette said. "To celebrate your safe return."

"After all, you will break a record." Mr. Dentalette laughed. "You'll be the first Dentalette who's not a tooth fairy!"

The mother robin spoke again. "I would be delighted to throw a party for the fast little fairy who saved Robbie. I haven't been to Fairyland in ages, but I have lots of cousins there. I'm sure they will insist on hosting a thank-you party!"

✳✳✳

The next day, everyone gathered in the meadow. Streamers hung from Mr. Willow's branches. He was so excited, he forgot to cry. Balloons floated in the air. Lightning bugs lit the sky with their fireworks. Robins, sparrows, and other birds fluttered around Belinda to hear her story.

"What's all the commotion?" asked Laurel, flying by. "Oh." She eyed the happy celebration. "It's just some silly birds. I heard all about your trip to Earth-Below," she said to Belinda. "You didn't even find the house. But now you think you're so great just because you saved one little robin."

"Well, we flowers think she's great," said Belinda's friend Daisy.

"And we do too!" exclaimed Dorrie, flying in with Trina and Olivia.

"So do we," chimed a chorus of birds.

"Hmmmph," said Laurel, and she flew away.

Belinda laughed. Then she hugged her friends one by one. "Thank you so much," she said. "If you hadn't helped my parents, I'd still be on Earth-Below."

"Belinda Dentalette stuck on Earth-Below? That would be terrible," Dorrie said. "Who would help me scatter fairy dust?"

"Who would be my rainbow painting partner?" asked Olivia.

"Who would joke about my books?" asked Trina.

Belinda grinned. "You're the best friends any fairy could have!"

"Roses are red, violets are blue, to help our friends, we stick like glue!" they recited together, holding hands.

"So, Belinda," Mr. Willow said. "What kind of fairy do you think you'll be now? A lightning fairy? A leaf-swirling fairy?"

"Well, you do need to be a fast flier for those jobs," Belinda answered. Then she clapped her hands. "But I have another idea." She laughed when her friends groaned. "I mean a really good idea this time.

"I will be," she announced, "a Go-to-School-and-Wait-and-See-What-Kind-of-Fairy-I-Want-to-Be Fairy!"

The Fairy School Pledge

(sung to the tune of "Twinkle, Twinkle, Little Star")

We are fairies
Brave and bright.
Shine by day,
Twinkle by night.

We're friends of birds
And kind to bees.
We love flowers
And the trees.

We are fairies
Brave and bright.
Shine by day,
Twinkle by night.

Fabulous Fairy Crafts!

Belinda, Trina, Dorrie, and Olivia have lots of fun at Fairy School, using special fairy tools. Here are some simple directions you can follow to create your own magical fairy stuff. All it takes for you to make fairy magic are a few special tools of your own—and a big imagination!

FAIRY WAND

You'll need:

Construction paper
A pencil
Scissors
Glue
Glitter
A straw or a Popsicle stick

• Decide what shape you'd like your fairy wand to have. It could be a star, a diamond, a heart, or a circle. Decide what color the wand will be too.

• Fold the piece of construction paper in half. Draw your favorite shape lightly on one side of the paper with the pencil.

• Cut through both pieces of paper so you have two identical shapes.

• Cover one side of each shape with a thin coating of glue.

87

Sprinkle glitter over the glue to make a sparkly wand. Wait 10 minutes for the glue to dry.

• Lay each shape down on its glitter side, with the plain side up. Spread a thin line of glue around the edge of the plain side of each shape.

• Carefully lay the straw or Popsicle stick on one of the shapes. The tip of the straw or stick should be in the middle of the shape. Place the other shape on top of the straw so that its edges are even with the edges of the other shape.

• Wait 5 to 10 minutes for the glue to dry, and *Ta-da!* Your very own fairy wand! Wave it around and see what sort of magic you can make happen.

STAR NECKLACE

On Belinda's first day at Fairy School, her mother gave her a star necklace to light her way home. People can't lasso shooting stars, but these directions will show you the next-best way to make your own star necklace.

You'll need:

A piece of thin white paper
A pencil
Scissors
Thin cardboard (from a clean milk carton)
Foil or metallic paper
String, leather cord, or ribbon

- Trace the star shape below on the white paper. Cut it out and use it as a pattern.

- Place the star pattern on the cardboard and trace the pattern lightly with the pencil.

- Use your scissors to cut out the star.

- Wrap the foil around the cardboard. Cover every spot so it's nice and shiny!

- Use the tip of your scissors to make a hole in the tip of one star-arm. Be careful!

- Thread your string, cord, or ribbon through the hole. Tie both ends of the string around your neck and you've got your very own star necklace! The light should look beautiful as it reflects in the foil.

FAIRY DUST AND FAIRY BAG

This one's easy!

You'll need:

Colored paper
A square piece of felt or scrap cloth, about 8 inches on all
  sides
A hole puncher
Ribbon or pretty yarn or string

• Find lots of fun pieces of paper. The more colorful, the
better! You can use stationery, construction paper, the comic
strips from the Sunday newspaper, even labels from canned
goods.

• Lay your cloth on the table where you'll be working. This
will become your bag.

• Start punching holes in the colored paper, over the cloth.
Keep punching until you have a big pile of dots. You should
have lots of colors to make your fairy dust especially magical.

• Pick up the four corners of the cloth and bring them together over the center of the pile. Tie a bow or piece of yarn
or string around the bag and you can carry your fairy dust
with you wherever you go.